JACK PERRY
AND THE
PIRATE PORTHOLE

CHRISTINE PERKINS

The right of Christine Perkins to be identified as the
Author of the Work has been asserted by her in accordance
with the Copyright, Designs and
Patents Act 1988

Jack Flynn and the Pirate Porthole © Christine Perkins 2019
Cover and illustrations © Terry Cooper 2019

Editor: Shaun Russell
Editorial: Will Rees & Lauren Thomas

Printed and bound in the UK by
Severn, Bristol Road, Gloucester, GL2 5EU

ISBN: 978-1-912535-06-4

Published by
Candy Jar Books
Mackintosh House
136 Newport Road, Cardiff, CF24 1DJ
www.candyjarbooks.co.uk

To George

For my mum, Valerie Hancox (1940-1990) whose talent in all things creative knew no bounds! I would like to think that I have captured her love of story and her 'voice' somewhere in these pages!

'Try puttin' it over your 'ead, Stringy!' said Crudge with a laugh. 'Make sure the door thingy is open before you do it though!'

'No!' A voice burst in from a particularly solid looking pirate. 'Try rubbin' it. You know, like Aladdin's lamp! That should do it!' He guffawed.

'I've got it. I've got it!' Slick, another of the motley crew, jumped up and down in excitement. 'I've got it. Put it on the deck. I'll show you!'

Slick was the deckhand. He had an **OILY** look. His face looked like it had never come into contact

1

with soap or water throughout his grubby piratey life! If he sat down, you could see where he'd been.

He took the *porthole* from Stringy Strong (a very tall and rather lean fellow, but a strong, experienced and trustworthy pirate all the same) and placed it on the deck.

The rest of the crew stood around **gawping** with their mouths open. Using exaggerated movements, Slick placed it down very carefully and warily opened the brass door, performing a little bow to his expectant audience as he did so. Not a sound could be heard as he lifted one of his bony legs

and placed his toes, like a ballerina, into the *porthole*. Some of the crew let out a jingling round of applause as he winched up his second foot and placed his big toe (which was visible through his rather holey sock) into the *porthole*. He lifted his arms as if he had scored a goal at a football match. The crew roared, even though he hadn't really done anything yet.

'Hoorah!' they shouted, laughing, clapping and cheering as Slick stood, arms raised, smiling a big gummy smile and enjoying the attention.

Then **WHOOSH** he disappeared.

For a second, the other pirates stared in awe, but soon they were running around, bumping into each other, trying to get a view of the *porthole*, which still lay open on the deck. A few of them were on their knees, scraping the deck with their dirty fingernails.

There was **NO** trap door. There were **NO** loose boards. There was **NO** Slick! He was...

NO more!

This was not the first time one of their crew mates had disappeared, but it was first time any of them had vanished through the floor!

But what of that first pirate? Well, it's probably best to start at the very beginning...

After a hard day looking for treasure, the crew returned to their pirate ship – **the Bones** – carrying several large wooden chests.

Stringy Strong was the first on board, carrying the heaviest treasure chest that he had ever lifted. As he put it on the deck, it began to jump around, as if there was a cat inside. *What in the name of Davy Jones' locker could be in it?* thought Stringy. Not being the bravest of pirates, he gave his cutlass to another pirate, Tommy Shivers.

Tommy took the cutlass and carefully edged towards the chest, which was still bouncing around the deck.

With one blow he **KNOCKED** the lock clean off!

Well… that was it!

The lid **SPRUNG** open as the men took several steps backward. Then, the contents of the treasure chest came tumbling out.

Whatever it was, it flew out of the chest like a rocket!

The object fired several metres up into the air with a mighty **swhoosh**. As quickly as it had shot up, it came thundering back down again. The men scattered, covering their heads, waiting for it to land. And land it did – it came down with no mercy! But then stopped abruptly just above the deck, hovered for a few seconds before hitting the floor. It was a brass *porthole. A real brass porthole!*

Eddy 'Scratch-it' Scumble, the oldest and wobbliest of the pirate crew, scratched his head and prodded the *porthole* with his broom.

Nothing.

Scratching his armpit, he prodded it again.

Nothing.

Stringy Strong, now back in charge of his cutlass, moved around it slowly. He eyed it up and down, wondering if he should call the cap'n. Before he could make up his mind, the cap'n appeared on the deck.

Eddy poked the *porthole* with his broom, lifting it up on the brush end. The broom disappeared into the *porthole*, sucking poor old Eddy in with it.

Schlupppp!

Gone! No broom. No Eddy! Just the *porthole* left spinning on the deck.

Within a few minutes, the *porthole* had swallowed a number of the astounded crew. One such crew member was 'Lumpy' Larry who disappeared while attempting to use the *porthole* as a hula-hoop. Then there was 'Unlucky' Herbert (he was indeed, very unlucky) who met a more watery fate. His decision to attach the *porthole* to the inside of his cabin had been misguided. After fixing it to the wall, he grinned. *I've beaten it,* he thought.

But then, all of a sudden, he was sucked through.

The captain paced up and down the deck. 'There *must* be a way to use this "magic" *porthole* to our advantage. To get us out of these 'ere monster-filled seas and get back what is rightfully ours. There just must be.'

And indeed there was.

Far away in a normal house, in an average street, was a run-of-the-mill looking family that were just beginning their holiday. Upstairs in a bedroom a *porthole* appeared.

The captain flopped through the *porthole* and onto the bedroom floor. *It looks like a ship, but not like a ship,* he thought. He took a look around. There was a comfy looking bed with the skull and cross bones on it. Besides this was a treasure chest. Was there any treasure inside? The captain edged towards it, then **dived** to the floor when he heard voices. He looked for an escape as the voices drew nearer. He quickly threw himself under the bed.

'Come on, Jack, take a look at your room,' said a woman's voice.

'Wow, how does Aunty Becky do it?' said another voice. Then he heard **SQUEALING** and **laughing**.

'Come on, Scoot.'

'Coming, Mum,' the other voice replied, but it was high-pitched.

Don't sound like no pirate, thought the captain. The voice and its owner left the room. This was it. Time to make a **sharp** exit! The captain threw himself back through the *porthole*, head first.

Thwack!

8

He landed back on the deck of **the Bones**. He was in one piece, at least. He lay on the deck and stared at the sea of faces looking down at him. He rubbed his head. 'Am I back on the good 'ole Bones? Am I? I don't never want to go back there again! You can't make me!'

'What did you see, Captain? Tell us! Was it a sea monster like Snagwort? Or was it one of them Witches of the Waves? You know them 'orrible floaty things?'

'No, no it wasn't anything like that. It was ch... ch... ch... chil-drun. 'Orrible little chil-drun! Yak!'

'Where's the *porthole*, Cap'n?' asked Cracker nervously, looking around him as if it was going to appear out of thin air anytime!

Which it did! **POP!**

Onto the deck.

Cracker turned to face the captain. 'Did this 'ere lad sound... well... clever like? You said he was reading books. That means he's clever, don't it?' The captain nodded in agreement.

'Right!' said the captain, thumping his boot on the deck. A **FLASH** of red and green **zipped** around his hat and landed on his shoulder. 'Right then, Cracker. This is what we are going to do...' The captain **grabbed** hold of the parrot, who squawked in disapproval at being man-handled. Before he could disapprove a moment longer, the captain whispered in his parrot ear and shoved him beak and feather through the brass window.

Schloooop!

The parrot was no more! He was on a mission, with orders from the captain.

'Only time will tell now,' said the captain 'Good luck, Cracker!'

— CHAPTER ONE —

It was the beginning of the long school holidays and Jack and his family were heading to the coast where his Aunty Becky lived. On the first Saturday after they had finished school the family climbed into the car prepared for all events: a packed lunch, first aid box, blankets, sleeping bags, suitcases, buckets, spades, sun cream and a car boot full of so many things that they probably wouldn't need – but Mum insisted!

Aunty Becky was Mum's younger sister, although you'd never have thought it if you saw them standing next to one another. They couldn't have been more different! Aunty Becky was an artist. She had wild, crazy-coloured hair and wore the **strangest** clothes sometimes, but one thing Jack and his sisters knew for sure was that she just loved it when they came to stay.

Her house was on quite a **steep** hill. It looked like every other house in the street, but when you stood in the porch you could just about (if you stood on your tip toes) see the sea.

And if you went upstairs to the front bedroom the view was **spectacular!**

A sparkling view of the beach, complete with a

glimpse of the big wheel and even the lighthouse in the distance.

Staying with Aunty Becky meant Mum and Dad would sleep downstairs, his two sisters, Molly and Scoot, would sleep in the big room at the back of the house and Jack would have the smaller room at the front. Jack was **always** pleased with this arrangement. It felt like he had his very own den.

There was always a pile of books scattered around that Aunty Becky would buy from car boot sales in the lead up to their visit.

There were adventure stories, science fiction, space, dragons and spy books. You name it; Aunty Becky would have a book just for you.

Jack, Molly and Scoot took their bags from the car. 'Come on,' said Aunty Becky. 'I've got a surprise for you this year!' She led them up the stairs.

CHAPTER TWO

'Beware all who enter this 'ere pirate cabin!' Jack read the sign that swung menacingly on the door.

'Wow!' Jack said under his breath. He opened the door nervously, biting his bottom lip. He pushed the door back and found himself standing inside the room. 'Oh, yes! **Ohhhhh Yesssss!**'

He was standing inside the cabin of a pirate ship!

Time for a high five, thought Jack, as he swung around and **high-fived** himself in the tall mirror standing in the corner.

How did Aunty do it? How *did* she do it?

He scanned the room. The windows were now yellow. They appeared to be covered in plastic film that made them look really old and well... *piratey!*

One window was slightly open and you could almost smell the ocean. The bed had high wooden sides to stop him from falling out in high seas. It was actually just painted cardboard, but it was **BRILLIANT**... Aunty was so clever!

His duvet was adorned with the skull and crossbones flag. Another hung on the back of the door. The breeze from the window buffeted the flag, making Jack feel as if he were already on the ocean waves.

On the wall, over the top of his bed, was a map. It wasn't a map of any country Jack recognised or that he had seen before. He thought carefully about the lessons he'd had at school: Great Britain, the Celts, the Vikings, the Victorians. No he didn't recognise it.

He moved a bit closer. 'The Walalama Islands? Nope. Never heard of them!' he said out loud.

In the corner of the room sat a large wooden box – a trunk, I suppose you might call it. It looked as if it weighed a ton, but its weight was only Jack's second thought. His first thought was **TREASURE!** His mind was buzzing, and in one step he was standing at the very edge of the box. A label was attached to the lid. It looked very old, was brown, dark around the edges but faded in the middle. *Just like a real pirate message*, Jack thought. On it was a message, which he duly read:

Measure for measure,
Keep your hands off this treasure.
So do not let your fingers linger,
My lily livered mate.
Take one morsel from this chest and
You will meet your fate.

Jack's hands hovered for a while over the lock. It was one of those times... Perhaps you've had that feeling yourself. You know you shouldn't touch something but you are drawn to it. It's like looking into a **big** hole, peering deep down into it and feeling as if you are going to fall in.

Jack's fingers brushed over the cool metal as he read the message again.

What does it mean? he thought. *What does "fate" mean?* Jack had no idea. 'Come on,' he mumbled. 'You're no scaredy cat.' He took a deep breath.

'Come on! Open it, open it!'

But the voice wasn't Jack's.

'Open it! Open it!' said the voice again.

Trying not to move a muscle in his body, Jack spun his head around like an owl. On the wall in front of him was a *porthole* – just like the ones you have on pirate ships!

That wasn't there before, he thought. There it was.

18

A perfect circle of brass and glass and through it Jack could see the sea. He gazed through the *porthole*, eyes like saucers in disbelief.

Then something flew at him!

It was a flash of red, green and possibly blue. Jack took a step back and almost fell over a plastic sword lying next to his bed. The *porthole* was pulsating, but that wasn't possible.

'Open it! Open it!' squawked a voice. It seemed to belong to a bird! Jack watched in total awe and well, **shock** really, as the multi-coloured, airborne spy swooped to and fro; *SQUAWKING, SWOOPING* and feathers flying, all at the same time. 'Open it! Open it! Jack's a scaredy cat. Jack's a scaredy cat!'

The bird flew up, down and sideways, echoing Jack's own words back at him. Jack leaned a little further out of the *porthole*, on tip toes now. He leaned as far as he could, but he couldn't quite fit his shoulders through it. He watched the bird **dip** and *dive*, and tried to keep up with its movements. The bird wasn't going to give up in a hurry.

'Jack's a scaredy cat! Jack's a scaredy cat. Won't open it! Won't open it!' The bird was so loud Jack was concerned that the whole neighbourhood might hear.

'Oh no you don't,' muttered Jack, as he launched himself out the door and down Aunty's stairs three at a time, leaving the skull and crossbones flag *waving* in the air as he went. A puff of pink fairy dust wafted out of Scoot's room with the jet of air he left behind.

He ran past Molly on the way down, who was on her mobile talking to one of her friends. 'Excuse *me!*' Molly said with a **huff**. 'Since when have I been invisible? Jack? I said, since when… huh! Brothers!' and went back to her conversation. Jack had more important things to deal with now than big sisters on mobile phones.

He reached the door, not stopping there; he seemed to move from the doorstep onto the grass in one full jump, landing with a **bump** on the front lawn. Immediately looking skyward, his eyes were scanning the area for "that bird".

Every now and then he would see a flurry of feathers, this way, then that; one red, one green. It was a blur, and it was actually making Jack feel quite **SICK**! Then, he caught sight of the feathered infiltrator.

It swooped down lower and lower, and with one final almighty low **dive**, the parrot seemed to cut through the air, up the garden path next door and in through the wide open front window.

Without giving it a second thought, Jack leapt over the fence that separated Aunty's garden from Ms McGinty's.

*

Ms McGinty was as old as her tongue and a little bit older than her teeth. That's what she would say if anyone asked her how old she was. She was very **NIMBLE** on her feet and didn't need a stick to walk, or anything like that. Her hair was like a big swoop of candy floss, but grey! It sat perched on top of her head and would **sway** in the breeze.

Sometimes she would perch a small green hat on top of her hair. And in the hat was a hat pin. Hat pins aren't used much these days so this must have been **VERY** old.

Just like Ms McGinty.

The pin itself looked like a big green jewel. Most people were unable to look at it without feeling hypnotised. If you stopped for a chat, you would find yourself being drawn to it, until Ms McGinty would say abruptly, 'Cheery-bye then.'

And then she would disappear, leaving the other person **OPEN-MOUTHED** and wondering what they had been chatting about.

There was certainly something about Ms McGinty that remained a MYSTERY, but what could be so mysterious about a little old lady with grey hair and a little green hat?

Jack followed the trail of feathers to the front window. He pushed his nose up against the glass for a closer look. He could, of course, have put his head inside the window, but Jack was far too polite for that. No, that would have been very **rude** indeed! He strained his eyes a little bit more, peering harder through the glass. 'Rats and double rats!' He couldn't see anything that looked feathered, red or green. Jack's curiosity got the better of him, and he put his head through the open window and looked around. He felt very **NERVOUS**. Most probably because he had his head stuck in the neighbour's front window. Still seeing nothing, he leaned in a touch further and with his feet barely on the grass Jack strained his neck until his shoulders were now in the window too. Just a bit more, until… a single, lonely, but oh, so tell-tale, tail feather floated silently down on to Ms McGinty's best carpet.

I have you now my feathered friend, thought Jack.

And before you could say "The bee's knees" Jack found himself standing inside Ms McGinty's front room with the red feather in his hand. He stood, **NERVOUSLY** moving the feather between his fingers, back and forth from his thumb and forefinger. He felt as if was being **watched,** the same feeling he had only minutes earlier in his room.

He edged round, first on his right foot, leaving his other foot in the same spot. His body moved before his feet did.

There behind him was a tall, old fashioned-looking bird cage. A bit like one you would see in books about "**THE OLDEN DAYS**". It was taller than Jack and he could just about touch the top of it if he stood on his tip toes, then stretched up a bit. It was gold and stood on four spread out, claw-like feet. On the front of the cage was a small door. Over the top of the door was a tiny sign that read:

'DO NOT OPEN THIS DOOR RARE PARROT!'

CHAPTER THREE

Jack's thoughts were tripping over one another. But, if the door isn't allowed to be opened, then how did this bird get out? And if it got out... Jack's head was full of unanswered questions. How did it get back in? Jack stared silently into the cage, pondering this thought carefully.

He looked **QUICKLY** and **puzzlingly** from the cage door to the window, to the parrot and then back to the window. How had the parrot done it?

'Open it! Open it!' the parrot squawked.

Jack's jaw dropped; his mouth open just wide

enough to **wedge** a mini doughnut in.

Perhaps Jack had imagined it. He shook his head, blinked his eyes and tried to clear his thoughts. He looked back at the parrot.

'Jack's a scaredy cat! Jack's a scardey cat!'

There was no mistake this time. The parrot had spoken to him. And it knew his name! Jack edged a bit closer toward the cage. Perhaps it's a trick, a radio controlled voice, someone standing behind the door. Jack searched hard for any explanation.

The parrot's eyes met Jack's eyes. 'Open it! Open

it!' it said.

Slowly Jack's hand started to move upward, floating almost. *I'm being hypnotised,* he thought. *This is ridiculous.*

His fingers moved slowly to the lock across the door of the cage, and slid the little bar up. Before you could say, "The flea's knees" Jack's fingers moved the catch up and...

CLICK!

The door opened effortlessly. As it swung back, it appeared to be in slow motion.

'Cracker's out! Cracker's out!' squawked the bird as it flew frantically around Ms McGinty's front room. In the blink of an eye, and the fluffing of a feather, Jack made a determined decision to leave the room. **NOW!**

So, as fast as his legs would carry him, he ignored the door and headed for the window.

The parrot, in the meantime, was still flapping

around the room as if there was a fire in his tail feathers.

I've let Ms McGinty's precious parrot out of that cage. Do not open, it said. What have I done?!

Jack **dived** towards the window, or where the window should have been. He couldn't believe what he was seeing. The window had turned into a wall and in the middle of the wall was a porthole! It was the same porthole that had appeared in his bedroom. Exactly the same! How would he get out of the room now? Jack felt a wave of panic flush through him. Hot then cold, then hot again. He bent down, defeated almost.

As he stood up, he felt a waft of air and a **flash** of red dart over him, practically shaving the hairs from his head. Jack watched in amazement as his trainers began to rise up from the floor. He was no longer standing on Ms McGinty's carpet, but instead his legs were dangling about a metre off the ground and, worse still, the ground was moving further and further away from his feet.

'Hey! What's happening? Put me down!' he cried.

The parrot had Jack's shirt in its beak. 'Hold on... hold on...' squawked the feathered fiend as Jack felt himself getting smaller and smaller.

'What's happening to me? Hey, I'm shrinking!' shouted Jack.

And before he knew it, Jack and the parrot had squeezed through the *porthole*, popping out the other side. Not only had Jack shrunk to the size of the small feathered pest, but they were flying **HIGHER** and **HIGHER** with each of Jack's demands for help.

'Put me down!' he pleaded.

The bird **screeched** as they flew through the air, over the roof tops. Jack continued to scream. It wasn't fun being held by his shirt in the beak of a small and quite frankly, mad parrot.

After some time, he decided to stop wriggling. The parrot seemed to have a firm grip and, quite surprisingly, he was enjoying the view. He watched as they flew over the sand dunes next to the little road that led to the sea. He could just about make out the small car park where Dad had parked before marching off to the beach.

His thoughts soon returned to the real world with a bang – a real

There it was again... **BANG!**

And again.

Jack squeezed his eyes shut and wrapped his arms around the bird.

Minutes later, he eased one eye open to see that the houses, roof tops, trees and the beach were gone. He was now flying over open sea.

The bird **screeched**, and with his feet still trailing behind his body, Jack scrunched his eyes to get a better look at the sea below him. His feet were being dragged through puffs of white smoke. He passed through them like little wispy cotton wool clouds. In between the trails of smoke, Jack could see the outline of a ship. He squinted a bit harder.

It was a large ship!

There was a picture on the flag that looked like…

BOOOOOM!

A small, but perfectly round hole appeared in the cloud of smoke just to the side of Jack's body. A cannon ball shaped hole in fact.

'Right, that's it!' yelled Jack. 'Put me down this very second. Do you hear me you crazy bird?'

Jack felt his body dip. You know the feeling... When the lift starts to move and your head stays where it is, but your stomach feels like it's dropped to your socks. **Eeeugh!**

Swooping below the clouds of smoke, Jack was heading straight towards the ship.

He gulped and looked again. **Oh yes!** He was sure of it now. It was the skull and crossbones. Sagging on the flag pole, black as night, the flag flapped sulkily to and fro, tattered and frayed around the edges. Jack swallowed hard. *Oh yes! That ship is a pirate ship – no doubt about it!*

— CHAPTER FOUR —

They moved closer to the ship until the parrot dropped Jack onto the deck with a thud. He lay there for a while, his eyes shut tight, scared to open them.

Slowly he opened one eye and, without moving his head, he scanned the deck. What would happen to a parrot-sized boy on a pirate ship? Jack remained still, not moving a muscle or a hair on his head. 'Normal size, normal size!' screeched the parrot.

'Landlubber ab-oard!' came a loud voice. 'Landlubber ab-oard!' There it came again, then again and again. Before you could **shake** a parrot feather, a normal-sized Jack was stood in front of about thirty or so (Jack was always quite good at estimating!) of the **SCRUFFIEST**, **dirtiest** looking men you could ever wish to set eyes upon. Jack's eyes moved up and down the group. **Pirates!** Every last one of them.

But where was the captain?

He couldn't see anyone that looked like the captain. None of the pirates had a hat. Or an eye patch. Or a parrot on his shoulder. There was no wooden leg. He scanned quickly down the line of pirates. They looked like pirate skittles waiting to be bowled over.

They're an ugly bunch if ever I've seen one, thought Jack, cringing. These men were, in fact, so ugly, so tatty and so filthy that there appeared to be a green **SMOLDERING** fog rising up from the tops of their heads.

One thing was certain, Jack had never seen anything quite like them before and it was also very clear that they had never seen anyone quite like him. Jack stared at the pirates. The pirates stared at Jack. This all took less than a minute, but it seemed to last a lifetime.

Jack was just beginning to think he must be in a time warp, another dimension. His gaze moved along the pathetic parade of pirates.

Suddenly there was a **FLASH!**

No, a **THUD.**

No, a **whoosh!**

Actually, it was all these things together.

And Jack found himself face down on the deck.

Cautiously, he looked up to find two black boots. They were so close to him that they were almost touching his nose. Jack could feel his heart **beating** and could feel a small trickle of sweat rolling its way down the back of his neck. His eyes traced the boots upwards, eventually arriving at a pair of bottle green, totally moth-eaten trousers. The trousers were tucked into the boots. One of the boots began tapping impatiently.

TAP, TAP TAP!

This made Jack nervous, but he was transfixed by the tapping boot.

Then, it came... an almighty roar!

So loud and so powerful, it was actually much louder than the explosion Jack had made with his chemistry set. And louder than his sister's scream when she found her doll covered in gloopy, purple goo.

That was how **loud** it was!

'What is this article of puniness, this watery weakling, doing on my ship?'

There was a strange silence that seemed to go on forever.

'Speak!' he roared. 'Who are you boy?' He roared again, laughing out loud this time. He grabbed Jack and moved his face closer. His breath smelt horrible! 'And more importantly why are you dressed like that? You are dressed in the **STRANGEST** garb I've ever laid me eyes on!' He plucked and pinched at Jack's new football shirt that his dad had bought him.

Jack felt his brain **thumping** inside his skull. He knew that if he opened his mouth to speak only silence would come out – if silence can do that! The hush lingered in the air. It seemed to swirl about for a few seconds before it was met with, 'Well?! I'm waiting, you scurvy dog!'

'Jack,' he croaked, when he eventually let out a small sound. 'Sir, er, Captain. My name's Jack Flynn.'

'Well, well, well, Jack Flynn you say.' The captain spoke slowly, emphasising each letter.

The crew were staring at him, as if they were waiting for something to happen, as if they were waiting for the captain to make some sudden move. Jack looked at the crew. They were edging back towards the side of the ship, ready to make a quick exit if the captain happened to turn on them.

Stifled mutters came from the tatty-looking pirates. Jack could hear words like "FOR THE CHOP", OR "PLANK", OR "GIZZARDS", OR "THROAT", and more worryingly "Overboard".

'The thing is, Jack m'lad. The thing is...' The captain waved his arm out to sea. 'We need your help.'

CHAPTER FIVE

The captain handed Jack a telescope. 'Have a look,' he said.

Jack could not see anything, except for an island far away in the distance.

'That, Jack m'lad, is why we are here. It's the reason we took the pirate's oath.'

Jack nodded, but he didn't have the slightest clue what the captain was ranting on about.

Cracker took a **swoop** from the Crow's Nest, from where he had been watching Jack. He landed smoothly on the captain's shoulder. A small green feather fluttered in the air. Jack watched the feather float back and forth, until it finally landed on the wooden deck.

'What the cap'n is trying to say—'

The captain interrupted, snatching the telescope from Jack. 'There's treasure on that island and we can't get our hands on it. Do you know why?' The captain paused for effect. Jack shook his head. 'Because there's a roaring great sea monster in the way!'

There was a **gasp** from the crew. Some covered their ears. Some covered their eyes. Then there was nothing, only the occasional gulp or swallow to break the silence.

'We left the treasure there many moons ago and now that darned sea monster won't let us get to the island and dig it back up!' squawked Cracker.

The crew nodded in agreement – all at the same time – as if they had practised it before. The word "monster" rumbled around the deck like a barrel full of bricks.

'The question is, Jack m'lad,' said the captain. 'What are we going to do about it?' The captain stomped up and down, down and up, pacing the boards.

Jack peered out to sea. Sure enough, he could see a dark shadow between the ship and the island, but he couldn't quite make out what the shape was.

'Ere, take the spy glass.' The captain shoved the telescope back in Jack's hand. 'Look there! That's what you're up against!'

Jack looked again at the eerie figure in the sea. He had never seen anything like this before... anywhere! He could make out the monster's head; a great bell shape **bobbed** up and down in the swell of the waves. Using the telescope, Jack followed the head of the monster down its long scaly neck and along its body. There was something he couldn't quite put his finger on. There was something, but what was it?

Jack turned the telescope back towards the head; the body was made up of four rounded humps. Then Jack noticed it and everything clicked.

The tail!

The monster had a tail shaped like an arrow. Jack watched as it disappeared under the black waves. Tranquilly the tail reappeared, but this time it wasn't arrow shaped, it was shaped like the end of a fork. Jack racked his brains to try and think of what this shape was called. He'd seen it in a history book at school. He stopped looking at the monster; his thoughts taking him back to school. He dug his hand into his pocket. Even though they were slightly melted, he still had five **Choccospheres** left.

What should he do now? It wasn't like he was normally faced with a two tailed sea monster on a ship full of pirates, with a **MAD** talking parrot and an unwashed stinking captain, who had obviously never visited a dentist. Jack had no idea, but he had the feeling that the captain was expecting him to have some kind of answer.

He looked around at the *shambles* of a crew. They weren't going to do anything that was for sure. They stood huddled together; eyes wide, knees knocking and what few teeth they had between them were chattering in fear.

Jack looked out to sea again, catching a glimpse of the monster bobbing up and down. He looked back at the captain. He gulped and bravely blurted out, 'What is it?'

'That!' spat the captain, 'is the Snagwort.' He **wiped** his nose on the back of his sleeve. Jack tried not to look. 'Snagwort, the most dreaded sea-dwelling monster of 'em all. Or so it is told. One thing's for sure, we ain't ever gonna get our treasure back with him roaming around that island.'

'Do you live there then?' Jack asked politely. The captain gave an **enormous** belly laugh. 'Hah! No, we don't live there. There's nothing on that island worth living there for. It's just a no-good piece of rock—' He tailed off, mumbling.

'Couldn't you just come back later? When the monster's not there?' asked Jack.

'Hah, we could, but we wants our treasure and we wants it **NOW**!' Replied the captain, slightly irritated.

The captain stepped closer to Jack. **TOO CLOSE!** Jack was now eye to eye, brow to brow and nose to nose with the stinking pirate. Jack **SQUEEZED** his eyelids tight and felt his toes curl up inside his trainers. *What would the captain do? Had he overstepped the mark?* He bravely opened one eye, ever so slightly. *Yep! He was still there.*

The captain inched in a bit closer and then – with barely a whisper – he said, 'Treasure.' The word slipped slimily out of his mouth. Almost **oozing**. 'Treassssssure.' He smiled as he said it quietly, tapping his finger on his nose.

'We need it!' came a squawk from above, as Cracker flew from the captain's shoulder and darted here and there with feathers flying. 'We need it! We need it!' he shrieked again. 'Treasure! Treasure!'

'Yes, I know you need it, but how can I help you? I've never even been on a pirate ship. Come to think of it, neither have I been shrunk, squeezed through a magic *porthole* or dragged through the air by a talking parrot.'

46

The captain shook his head. 'Oh no, Jack m'lad. That's where you're quite wrong. You're not going to fight the Snagwort. You are going to **feed** him! Ha, ha, ha, ha, ha!' The captain obviously found this very amusing. 'Fish food. That's what you're going to be, laddie! Fish food! A lickle bit of bait to take the Snagwort's eye off our treasure.'

The crew seemed to be enjoying his misfortune. Jack gulped as they **whooped** and rubbed their hands together in complete glee.

'Silence!' snapped the captain. 'Be no good me throwing one of my crew overboard now, would it? Not much going for 'em is there? Mangy lot! Oh no! Jack you are just what the cap'n ordered. You're of fine stock, there's no doubt.'

'What do you mean?' said Jack with a tremble.

'What I mean is that you, you scrawny piece of fish food will walk the plank, just in time for Snagwort's dinner. And whilst he's nibblin' on your lickle pinky toes...' He turned and threw his arm around in the direction of the crew. 'We will sneak the good old **"Bones"** around the back of the island. Genius! That's what it is!'

Cracker flew overhead. 'Genius. Genius. Fish food Jack! Genius. Genius. Fish food Jack!' he sang. The crew joined in and were dancing around the deck, swinging each other round by the elbows, with Cracker darting in and out of them.

— CHAPTER SIX —

Jack's mind was **WHIRRING** like helicopter blades. He was going to be tossed overboard as fish food. *What should he do?* His head hurt from thinking and he found himself staring out to sea; his gaze meeting the island and the horizon.

'But you can't. You just *can't* do that! I wouldn't be much of a distraction. I wouldn't trick the monster. I'm not very meaty… er, I'm just not... I'm not a good swimmer!' (Jack was actually a very good swimmer.) The words **tumbled** out of his mouth in a hopeless attempt to avoid him being tipped overboard, and into the Snagwort's mouth. 'Look.' He **pinched** the muscles in his upper arm. 'There's really not much meat on these puny things.' They were a bit on the skinny side, it must be said.

The captain carried on laughing. 'Too late, lad. It's been decided – you're going in! We just have to work out the best way to do it! Cracker?'

Before Jack could blink, Cracker took hold of Jack's shirt and once again lifted him into the air, with his feet **dangling** over the deck. In a feeble an attempt to free himself, Jack shook his legs.

'It's no good flappin' like a bird, Jacky boy. Cracker? You know what to do!'

50

With his legs dangling, Jack felt the deck move further and further away from his feet. He watched as the crew's faces all turned skyward, their toothless mouths open as they watched Jack and Cracker soar into the air.

As their faces became a blur, Jack could just about make them out: **CLAPPING, CHEERING** and

LAUGHING.

'Say hello to the Snagwort from us!' came a shout. Their voices trailed off until the captain and crew look liked little specks below on the ship.

'Well,' said the captain. 'Let's get a move on. That's the last we'll see of that lad. And with a bit of luck, the last we'll see of the Snagwort. Turn the ship around, starboard side! Man the canons! Hoist the main sail! Crudge, you watch the Snagwort!'

'Aye aye, Captain,' they all hollered back.

The crew (even though they were very dim) did as they were instructed, while the captain returned to his cabin, shutting the door behind him.

At the far end of his cabin, was a large wooden cabinet and on each side were identical carvings of wooden parrots. On the left-hand side, the captain grabbed hold of the parrot's wooden beak, pulling it toward him. The centre panel in the cabinet opened and split into two halves. It revealed a map of the island with the initials WtW on it, as well as an X. He stared at the initials and made a low snarling sound. In true pirate fashion, an X marked the spot where the treasure was buried. The captain placed his bony finger on the X.

'Oh, my beauty. You'll soon be mine – not long to wait now. The boy will be a cracking distraction for the Snagwort and we will take what's ours. Well, not exactly ours, but we'll get what we want and everything will fall into place.' He stared at the map.

The captain's thoughts turned towards Jack. 'So help us all, that boy had better get this right.'

The ship weighed anchor on the other side of the island. The seas were calm and blue and, promisingly, there was no sign of the Snagwort. **NOT A GLIMMER**. They could go ashore.

But the Snagwort had **not** disappeared. It was still lurking in the murky depths of the ocean. Only this time he was not alone. The waves bounced Jack up and down like a bad tempered horse in a rodeo. 'Wahey! Do that again!' the boy yelled.

The Snagwort lifted his tail up high, flicking it gently back into the sea, creating a ripple-like effect on his body – scales, humps and all! As the creature's back surged **up** and **down**, Jack was flipped **HIGH**, only to be caught by the Snagwort's tail.

It's just like a fishy baseball glove, thought Jack.

And he couldn't get enough of it, **laughing** and **screaming** the higher he was flipped. Jack wrapped his arms around the friendly creature. The pirates had absolutely no idea what the Snagwort was really like. They didn't know him at all!

Earlier, after Jack had found himself on the Snagwort's back, he sat pondering as whether or not the creature actually knew he was there.

He decided to test a theory. Holding on quite tightly to the beast he reached into his pocket for his Choccospheres.

Perfect!

He waved the chocolate beneath the beast's huge nostrils. The creature stirred.

This better work, thought Jack. *Or I'll be fish food.*

The Snagwort turned its head towards Jack. The dragon-like creature looked like a dog begging for food.

Jack grabbed a handful of the Choccospheres and tossed them into the beast's cavernous mouth. The chocolate balls rolled around the creature's teeth like a pinball machine and then, one by one, dropped onto Snagwort's long green tongue.

The creature's eyes **bulged** as the flavour hit his taste buds. This was a new sensation for the Snagwort and he appeared to be enjoying it; his tail slapping the sea with joy.

'Here we go again!' shouted Jack. 'Woo hoooo!

You're the best Snagwort ever!'

The captain was feeling very pleased with himself, almost smug. **HIS PLAN HAD WORKED.** But where was Cracker? The captain looked at the map, turning it upside down. And, more importantly, where was the treasure?

The captain was not very good at reading maps! Not like Cracker. He was the best map reader of all the seven seas.

What do I do once I have the treasure? He thought, as he paced up and down his cabin.

'I'm just not very good at this stuff. Trying to be 'orrible and all that! How I wish—'

The door of his cabin blew open and in stumbled Crudge.

'What is it, Crudge?'

'We are ready to go ashore, er, Cap'n.'

The captain took the map from the cabinet and

rolled it up. He pulled the parrot's beak down and the cabinet closed.

'Right-o! Let's get this done!'

About twenty of the crew followed the captain as they explored the sand dunes. They sang as they strode over the sandy lumps and bumps.

Measure for measure, we'll have our treasure.

Our fingers won't linger, I'm telling you mate

We'll soon have our treasure,

for that is our fate.'

They marched on, shovels over their shoulders. As they **stamped** through boggy marshes, into thick bramble bushes and out on to the grassy swamps, they sang their hearts out. **UNTIL...**

'Halt! Stop right here!'

THE SINGING STOPPED.

The captain sniffed the air around him, and with one upwardly pointing finger he ordered the men, 'Start digging, boys!' He pointed at the muddy ground below their boots.

The men wasted no time in putting their shovels to work. The sun was **high** in the sky as they continued to dig. The captain paced up and down, keeping one eye on the men and one on the sky. He needed to keep his eye out for Cracker.

'Where is that blasted bird?' he asked. 'Something tells me all is not well.' He stared at the clouds. 'There's a bad smell 'ere, and it's *not* Crudge's boots!'

— CHAPTER SEVEN —

The captain paced up and down, the **hot** sun beating down on him. As he watched the men dig, his mind began to slip back to "the good old days" when he was a poor deck hand. **The Bones** had been fun back then. He and the crew always seemed to be **LAUGHING** and **SINGING**. The good ole "cap'n" certainly knew how to run a good ship. 'Yes, good times were had under Cap'n Cr—'

'Shiver me timbers, sir!' shouted Stringy Strong, interrupting the captain's trip down memory lane. 'We've only gone and hit gold!'

The whole crew rushed over to him. He was stood in his moth-eaten pantaloon trousers and matching moth-eaten tunic. He **grinned** from ear to ear. Well, it was a grin of sorts – just not many teeth to show for it!

Stringy Strong leaned over and picked up a soil-covered box. He blew the dirt off. There was a plaque screwed to the top. It read:

THIS BOX BELONGS TO MS EMILINE FRANCES MCGINTY

It was quite a large box, made of the most beautiful wood. It had parrots and flags carved into the lid. On closer inspection, the flags were skull and crossbones. The captain cleared the rest of the dirt away with his already **filthy** hand. He read the plaque.

Underneath, was one more sentence:

DO NOT OPEN!'

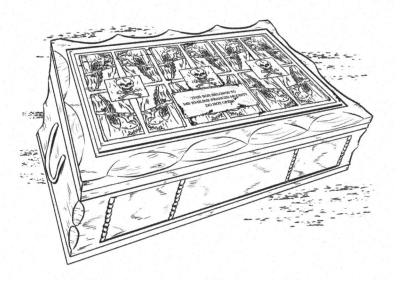

The captain looked pale and nervous.

'Go on, Cap'n,' said Stringy Strong.

Slowly, the captain lifted the lid as the **SCRUFFY,** rag-tailed crew watched, their mouths wide open. No one dared to talk, not even whisper. The captain took his cutlass and, very carefully, began to ease the lid off. He had a **good** idea as to what treasures lay inside the box. If he was right, those treasures were *the answers* to all their wishes.

As the captain carefully inched the lid apart there

was a ppfff sound – it was a bit like the noise your sandwich box makes when you open it. This was followed by an airy **gasp** from the surrounding crew, who had crept closer during the lid removal.

There it was! The very thing they had been looking for!

Now the captain knew what he had to do. He pulled out his telescope and **FOCUSED** on a green dot on the horizon.

Swooping and darting on the sea breezes, being tossed this way and that by the gusty winds, Cracker had the captain in his sight. He came **diving** down like a paper plane in full flight and landed right on top of the treasure box.

'Cracker, we've done it! We've only gone and done it! Beautiful, brilliant, booty! Did you...?

'Cracker did it! Cracker did it! Dropped him! Dropped him! Snagwort! Snagwort!' he squawked as he hopped around. 'Dropped him! Dropped him!'

Cracker did a **victory** fly past around the captain's mouldy old hat, landing on his shoulder.

The crew picked up their shovels and followed the captain and Cracker back to the ship. The men sang loudly as they **trampled**, **trudged** and **TRAMPED** back through the forest, swamps and grass and boggy marshes until they reached the sand dunes. Their singing got **LOUDER** and **ROWDIER** as they climbed the sandy slopes.

The captain reached the top first, with Crudge and Stringy Strong close behind. Anchored in the cove was their ship, but not all the crew noticed. They were enjoying themselves too much in a "party-like" conga line.

As the crew approached the top of the dunes they all bumped into each other, with the lead pirate stopping short at the top so that he did not go over the edge. They looked like a row of **scruffy** dominoes, knocking each other down one by one.

63

They all **BURST** out laughing as the captain tried to regain order.

'It's no time to be acting like a bunch of **NINCOMPOOPS** you 'orrible lot! We ain't back on the ship yet!' He pointed a dirty finger towards it. As he did so he did a double-take. There, bobbing up and down, and as clear and day, was the Snagwort! And it was between them and the ship!

There was no way they were going to get back now. Not with the Snagwort blocking the way! The captain's mind was *racing*. They had finally managed to recapture the treasure and now this! His jaw dropped to the buckle of his belt! His mouth **GAPING** like a great sea cave!

He squinted, trying to process the information. How? Surely not! Cracker had said. Cracker had most definitely said. There was no doubt about it! The bird had dropped that darned boy into the sea, right into the Snagwort's open jaws!

The captain blinked. Incredibly, Jack Flynn was sitting on the Snagwort's neck, right between the shoulder blades.

Not fish food!

NOT BAIT!

NOT CHEWED!

Or even a teensy weensy bit nibbled! No! He was most definitely in one piece!

'Crew get your muskets and cutlasses at the ready!' shouted the captain.

CHAPTER EIGHT

'It's OK, Cap'n!' hollered Jack. 'It's OK to come aboard. He won't harm you!'

The monster swam gently around the side of the ship. Jack was clearly having a great time riding the Snagwort, as it **dipped** and **dropped** him into the sea.

The crew couldn't believe what they were seeing. Was it really safe to row back to the ship?

'Come along, you 'orrible lot. Back to the ship!' They all grabbed the oars and rowed as fast their scrawny bones would take them.

The captain was the first up the ladder, followed by the rest of the crew. They looked like ants crawling up a honey-coated stick! Once on deck, the captain took out his telescope once again and focused it on the Snagwort. The monster and Jack were still **bobbing** up and down in the waves.

'What in the blue blazes is going on 'ere?' snorted the captain. 'How comes you're not fish food?'

'When Cracker **dropped** me I fell straight onto the Snagwort's neck, not in his mouth as you had asked him to do.'

The captain **SNORTED** again, muttering under his breath out of ear shot of Cracker. He never did like taking orders.

'The Snagwort didn't notice me at first, so I searched through my pockets for something to distract him. I couldn't find anything until I remembered I had some Choccospheres left.'

'Choccospheres? Chocc-o-spheres? What in

the name of Davy Jones are Choccospheres?' The captain shook his head, his eyes becoming wider and wider.

'These!' Jack reached into his pocket and took out an empty packet.

'What have these Chocco-spears-thingies got to do with not being eaten by the Snagwort?'

'I'm getting to that bit. I flicked a Choccosphere ball at his head to distract him. I was aiming for his eye but I missed. It went straight into his mouth. He seems to like them.'

The captain put his hand to his head. 'I'll be blowed. Choccospheres, eh?'

'He's quite gentle really,' said Jack, wrapping his arms around the Snagwort's neck.

'You'd better climb down from there, Jack m'lad. I think you've earned the whole story. Wouldn't you say, Cracker?

'Whole story! Whole story!' Cracker flapped

around the deck, red and green feathers fluttering to the ground.

The Snagwort carefully lowered its great bell-shaped head onto the deck of the ship. The crew **gasped** in horror as its wet nose touched the boards. Its small shiny, yellow eyes scanned the men.

Jack **slid** down the Snagwort's neck and landed gently on the deck. He turned and patted its head. With just one nod, he disappeared over the side and into the sea, leaving a few **ripples** in his trace, his arrow-shaped tail the last to enter the water.

And he was gone.

Jack ambled over to the captain. 'What's the whole story then?'

'It's like this. As hard as it is to imagine. I am…' He tripped over his words as he began to explain. 'I… I… I am not the really the cap'n of this 'ere ship. There I've said it!'

Cracker continued to fly and swoop over the crew.

'It's Cr-Cr-Cap'n Carruthers Cracknell! He's the cap'n. It's him! Cracker!'

The feathery **FUSSPOT** came to land on the captain's shoulder.

'Many years ago Cap'n Cracknell 'ere came across one Emiline McGinty. She was a fair beauty, that she was. Sharp as a cutlass! She was brave an' all. She had travelled all over the world, collecting treasures a-plenty, kept 'em in box – a great **big** treasure chest!' He tapped the top of the chest with his **grimy** bony finger. 'There wasn't a place on the seven seas she hadn't visited. Not a city, town or village she hadn't seen.'

The crew listened intently. It was a tale the men never grew tired of hearing.

'Go on. Don't stop now!' urged Jack.

'Where was I? Ah, yes. We had been through a **terrific** storm. It was terrible. Almost as if something was trying to stop us from coming ashore, but mercifully we made it back to dry land. We had docked in a port like no other. There was something **magical** about it. Something mysterious, but it was *not* a welcoming port, you can say that for sure.' His eyes drifted about from side to side. He looked as though he was deep in thought.

Cracker coughed (if parrots can cough of course) 'A-hem!' he squawked.

'As you know all pirates love a good arm wrestle and Cap'n Cracknell saw a sign for a com...compo...compastish...oh well, you know a contest!'

'COMPETITION!' The crew (and Jack) all shouted.

'Aye, a com...compo... compost... one o' them. That's all he needed – **a dare!** There was nothing we could do to stop him.'

'He went to the tavern that very night to take part, and by the time we all arrived the crowds were beginning to gather.' The crew nodded in unison to confirm the captain's tale. 'The lights were **dim** and there was a fair ol' smell of rum and sawdust around the place – a real pirates den it was. Then Cap'n Cracknell took his seat and waited for his opponent to arrive. It was like time stood still. You could see the very air moving an' swirlin' all around that dingy place. **TICK, TOCK**!' The captain moved closer to Jack, his breath so bad that Jack coughed. 'Well, Jack m'lad. T'was a lady! Cap'n Cracknell was staring across the table at one Emiline Frances McGinty.'

I know plenty of girls in my class who have a go and win at arm wrestling, thought Jack. He nodded, 'Go on,' he said.

'Emiline Frances McGinty was indeed a **champion** arm wrestler of the highest degree and she had certificates to prove it! No person, pirate or otherwise, had *ever* beaten her. And so the contest began. It was the best of three matches. I am afraid to say that Cap'n Cracknell only made it to two.

'She beat him fair and square. He was just about to walk away and then he saw it. **IT WAS THE TREASURE CHEST!** It went everywhere with her."One more round?" said Cap'n Cracknell to Emiline. "Winner takes all! You win, you keep it. I win, I *take* it!" You could hear his laugh roll around and bounce off the walls of that stinky ol' tavern. "Deal!"said Emiline.'

— CHAPTER NINE —

Jack listened in awe as the captain's story unfolded. The captain continued, 'No sooner had Cap'n Cracknell **plonked** himself down than Emiline had his arm locked. They pushed each other to and fro, **grunting**, growling, until our "too clever for his own stinkin' boots" cap'n had other ideas. He wasn't going to be beaten by no woman. His tunic was a moth eaten-old thing; still 'ad the moths in it! He shook his dusty tunic and sure enough a couple of moths flew out. Cap'n Cracknell gave a **SHORT**, **strong** blow and a moth flew straight into the face of his opponent Ms McGinty. It landed right on the end of her nose! That was that, as far as the contest was concerned!'

'OVER!'

'Ended!'

'Before Ms McGinty's elbow had chance to touch the table in defeat, Cap'n Cracknell grabbed the treasure box and made his way – crew in close pursuit, back to our ship. Only one winner you would think, eh Jack?'

Jack nodded, **INTRIGUED** by the unfolding story.

'Ah, but Ms McGinty had one more trick up her very neat sleeve. No one saw it coming, that's for sure. As Cap'n Cracknell ran for it as fast as his bony legs would take him, Ms McGinty came out of the darkness and there, just above her head, appeared a shiny brass porthole.

'She lifted her hand towards it and BOOM!'

'Emiline Frances McGinty shot a cannonball at him.'

'Right out of the *porthole*!'

'From thin air!'

'It landed right on the back of the Captain's bonce.' The captain pointed to his head. 'He was knocked out cold, and we just stood and stared at him, still wondering where that darned *porthole* and cannonball came from. There was certainly no ship in sight, that's for sure! And then before our very eyes, I tell no lie, Jack, he fair disappeared! Like the **cannonball** coming out of thin air, it was incred-u-lous. We didn't know what to make of it. "Where's my treasure box?" demanded Ms McGinty. We looked around, but it was nowhere to be seen. It later transpired that Wally the Weasel, Crudge and Stringy Strong had picked up the box and done a **runner**. As you can imagine, Ms McGinty was not happy, oh no. I asked her where Cap'n Cracknell was. "What have you done with him?" I shouted. She tapped her shoulder and a green parrot landed on it. "This." She pointed at the parrot. "Is your scheming, cheating, no good, fibbing Captain Carruthers Cracknell! And he will remain a parrot – my parrot in fact – until my treasure is returned to **me**. She swung around looking at the line of men, each one going weak at their bony knees.

And with that Ms McGinty and Cap'n Cracknell disappeared. Today, Jack m'lad is the first time we have set eyes on Cap'n Cracknell for many years. We've sailed the seas looking for Ms McGinty and the Cap'n, we really 'ave.'

Cracker, or should we say Cap'n Cracknell was circling the captain's head. 'Take it back!' he squawked. 'Take it back right now! I want to stand in my own two boots again. I'm fed up with feathers.'

'Set sail,' roared the captain to the crew. They did as they were told, **bumping** into each other like balls in a pinball machine. 'Come on Cap'n Cracknell, you know what you have to do; one last flight with our good friend, Jack.' The captain pushed the chest towards Jack with his feet.

Cracker **swooped** low over the captain's head and then over the top of Jack's head. Still squawking and grumbling, the parrot took hold of Jack's collar and **HOISTED** him up into the air, treasure box and all. Jack had that shrinking feeling again.

'Oh no, here we go again!' Once again Jack was flying, holding onto the treasure box for dear life.

Looking at his feet being **BLOWN** around, Jack could see the sand dunes, followed by the pier, and then he spotted Aunty Becky's house. He couldn't wait to be back on solid ground.

REAL GROUND!

Aunty's ground!

With a bump, he landed outside Ms McGinty's

house. As they squeezed through the porthole and into Ms McGinty's front room, Cracker let out a strange **squawk**. Jack looked around desperately because: a) he wanted to get rid of the treasure box and b) he wanted to get out of Ms McGinty's house before being seen.

He **SCANNED** the room quickly – the living room door was open. He grabbed the handle to close it. His eyes flitted around the room and found the cage. Incredibly, Cracker was already in it!

Jack breathed a sigh of relief. He looked at the big mirror on the wall and then around the room again. *Mm, something is missing,* he thought. *What is it?* He wracked his brain. **The bird cage!** It wasn't there anymore. With his heart pounding and his head **thumping**, he spun around on his toes. In its place was a wooden cabinet with two carved parrots on the sides. It was very familiar, he'd seen this somewhere before. There was a tray on the top – just the same size as the box.

Jack placed the chest on the tray and blinked. He was sure that one of the parrots winked at him as the treasure chest was returned to its rightful owner.

Jack did not waste a moment. He left the house the same way he'd come in, through the window, hoping that a *porthole* wouldn't magically appear again.

He **jumped** onto the grass, over the fence, up the path and then up the stairs, shutting his bedroom door behind him with a thud! He went to the window to check that no one had seen him.

He fell onto his bed; eyes wide open, just staring at the top of his bunk. He looked at the **pirate** flag that Aunty Becky had pinned to the door and to the **TREASURE** map she'd placed on the chest.

'What a day!' he said aloud.

He went over to the open

window. A small green feather gently floated into his room. Jack picked it up and stared at it, the wispy bits moving as he breathed on it.

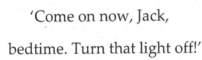

'Come on now, Jack, bedtime. Turn that light off!'

Jack was back and nobody had noticed. As instructed, he turned the light off. It was one of those **pirate** lamps used on ships. Aunty Becky was good, everything was just right.

'How did she do it?' he murmured to himself as he drifted off to sleep thinking of Emiline Frances McGinty, Snagwort, Crudge, Stringy Strong, Wally and last but not least, that darn bird, Cracker!

And in the distance, if you stood on your tip toes, you could if you **SQUINTED** make out the outline of a ship in full sail, being steered by one Cap'n Carruthers Cracknell. And following behind, like a faithful puppy, was a Snagworty-shaped shadow bobbing in and out of the water.

'Is that light off now, Jack?'

'Yes, Cap'n.' He yawned slowly, as he fell asleep to the sound of the ocean.

— EPILOGUE —

Three months later, the daily December smattering of Christmas cards dropped through the letter box and onto the Flynn's family door mat. However, today there was an **UNUSUAL** looking envelope amongst them. This one was addressed personally to Jack. More peculiarly, there was a green mist steaming out of it. Mum didn't notice, but Jack did, and what's more, he knew where he had seen it before.

Jack opened the letter and began to read…

83

Deer Jak m'lad

Coz we is pyrits we aint no gud at ritin and stuff so
we ope yoo can reed this messig awl rite.
We have had enuff of this ere port ole and have sent it
to yoo.

Me and Slick yoozed it first. It took us to the Norf Pole.
Shiver me timbers! It wos cold. Well... we had a bit of
a acksident – Slick fell throo the port ole and landed
head first on to the Norf Pole and snapped it in two!

Jimbo tried it next, throo the port ole he went, rear end
first, found himself sittin rite on top of one of them
pirimids in Egipt. Well once one brick started to topple
the rest of the briks came down with it. That pirimid is
no mor!

Stringy had a neer miss when he went throo it. He
found himself fallin' into a volcano – Ooo it was 'ot!
Poor Stringy burnt his 'yoo know what' on them
burnin flames. Sending him shootin up and out of that
firey pit! Like a pirit rocket he wos!

Old Tommy Shivers wos next to try it. He had no luck
either! Well at least we don't think he did. He's yet to
return to the Bones in fact. Goodness only knows where
he is?

So Jak, me and me crew had a parley – that meens a

talk – we decided that our luk wiv the port ole has runned out! We awl agree that yoo be the rite man for the job. The job of looking after the darned thing that is! Yooz it wizely Jak! As yoo can see it 'as shrunk to a tiny little port ole. That was not an eezy thing to do! Old Stringy has out of the kindness of his heart, given yoo his best bootlace. Yoo can keep it round your nek and yooz it whenever yoo want to. Yoo is clever aint yoo Jak? Yoo will know how to yooz it proper. But a wurd of warning – do not looz it. We carnt have it fallin into the rong hands now, can we?

May the gud fotune of the Bones be with yoo young Jak m'lad. I hope yoo have mor luk than we did.

Your Captin

PS If you see Old Tommy Shivers on yor travels try sending him bak to the Bones throo that blasted port ole!

And with that, Jack took the tiny porthole out of the envelope, threaded it onto the bootlace and then placed it carefully over his head.

JACK FLYNN

WILL RETURN

Christine Perkins has loved writing from an early age. Her stories have always contained a bit of 'magic' or mystery – witches, genies, wizards, spells, wands, magic potions, elves, pixies, toys that came to life, you name it!

Christine lives with her husband and has two grown-up sons. She says: 'They must be grown-up as they have beards, but they are not pirates!'

Although Christine doesn't have any pets, she does have a mad pheasant that roams the garden called Frankie, who in turn is stalked by a neighbour's cat called Buster!

On leaving school, Christine worked in a bank, but had secretly always wanted to teach, so when her own sons started school, so did she! Christine went to university in Birmingham to become a teacher. Today she is a deputy head in a primary school.

When she's not teaching, she enjoys travelling with Mr Perkins and their friends to far flung places and also to near flung places. She enjoys trying different foods, trying other languages (including pirate!) and walking, especially if Harvey (her son's giant pooch) is staying.

Fun facts:

- Christine's favourite superpower is flying.
- She likes a laugh.
- She is allergic to nuts.
- She cannot sew!

- She is a qualified yoga teacher.

- She doesn't know any pirates.

- She has a brother called Rob.

- She loves a fancy dress party/murder mystery.

- She makes a good trifle!

- She has never met a pirate or been on a pirate ship. Christine says, 'Oh yes I have! I went on the pirate ship ride at a theme park when I was eighteen and vowed never to go on one ever again! Being on the petite side, I nearly fell through the safety bars. Never again!'

Pirate jokes

Q: Why does it take pirates so long to learn the alphabet?
A: Because they can spend years at C.

Q: What subject are pirates best at at school?
A: Arrrrt.

Q: How do pirates prefer to communicate?
A: Aye to aye!

Q: How do ye turn a pirate furious?
A: Take away the 'p'.

Q: What did the pirate say when he blew the candles out on his 80th birthday?
A: Aye Matey (I'm eighty).

Q: What did the ocean say to the pirate?
A: Nothing, it just waved.

Q: What is a pirate's favourite Star Wars character?
A: AARRRRGGH-2 D-2!